VICTIM 087

ARYAN KUSHWAHA

notionpress.com

INDIA · SINGAPORE · MALAYSIA

ISBN 979-8-88883-936-2

Contents

Acknowlegdement

I would like to express my deepest appreciation to my parents and my school, Sir Padampat Singhania Education Centre, Kanpur. My school has not only provided me with the fellowship under the scheme of Smt. Manorama Govind Hari Singhania Fellowship for Aspiring Authors but also nourished me with encouragement and patience throughout this project. My mentors at school motivated me to print this book and reach out to everyone. Their invaluable contribution, suggestions, knowledge and relentless support are just a few things that helped me in the completion of my book.

I express my heartfelt gratitude to the Principal ma'am, Ms Bhawna Gupta and my English teacher, Ms Anila Chandak, the mentors behind this book who need special mention. Their reviews throughout my writing journey enabled me in bringing out the best.

This book won't be complete without mention of my parents Mr. Vijay Kumar Kushwaha and Mrs. Mira Kushwaha. Their contribution can never be overestimated.

Foreword

 *Sir Padampat Singhania Education Centre*
Kamla Nagar, Kanpur - 208 005, Uttar Pradesh (INDIA)
Affiliation No. 2130075 

December 16, 2022

FOREWORD

From the first time I met Aryan Kushwaha at school, I knew he was going to be a star. The writings in this book will surely help an individual to witness the elements of suspense and thrill from the young author's perspective in a distinct manner altogether. Each chapter is beautifully and intricately woven between the lines. The message can differ from person to person. After reading the chapters, I am sure the readers would be surprised that the author is just a fifteen-year-old.

Wishing you the best Aryan, for every step in your journey...Go and conquer your dreams... May God Bless you in all your endeavours.

Bhawna Gupta
Principal

website: www.spsec.co.in, email: school@spsec.co.in
Ph. No.: +91 512 2218222, 9235444858, Fax No.: +91 512 2218283

Episode 1

Getting Infected

Arjun Pandey was coming back to his childhood home in Kanpur to meet his childhood friends. He was a pilot of a fighter jet. He took a leave for a month. His flight landed around midnight. He fell asleep mid-flight. A flight crew member woke him up. He left the flight after everyone had left. He left the airport and found almost no one because everyone else took all the cabs and there was no cab available for him. He walked half a mile away in search of a cab. He was walking on a lonely street in the middle of the night and not even a single vehicle could be seen in a mile radius. He was very excited to meet his friends. The last time he met them was four years ago, before he and his sister Aranya went to the US to get settled.

Suddenly, he heard the sound of gunfire and immediately the CCTV (on the lamppost nearest to Arjun) was damaged by a gun bullet. He saw a van coming towards him. He got blinded for a couple of moments by the headlights of the van. The van hit Arjun at great speed and made him unconscious on the spot. He was lying on the road unconscious after the collision. Two men came out of the van. One of them checked the pulse rate of the body. The man showed his thumb up to indicate that Arjun was not dead but unconscious. The other man understood the signal and they both picked up Arjun's body and shoved him into the van where three bodies were already lying.

In those days, a pharmaceutical corporation named 'Raincoat' was the second richest company in the world. Three years ago, Raincoat came into existence. The logo of the company constituted two white triangles and one white parallelogram forming a bigger triangle. The logo signified 'unity in diversity'.

The company was founded by Avantika Sharma—a girl from a middle-class family. She possessed outstanding entrepreneurial skills because becoming the owner of the second-richest company in the world wasn't a piece of cake. Her corporation gave jobs to only women. Except for some security personnel, anyone working in Raincoat was a woman. Within no time, she became a well-known entrepreneur. Many people believed that she had faced gender discrimination in her dream job, which was the reason she only hired women. But there was always a possibility that she was doing it for the welfare of society.

Behind the scenes, something far more sinister and clever was going on. To test their projects, Raincoat used living human bodies. These people were made unconscious by a van accident and then brought to the Human Experiment Centre (HEC). Raincoat told everyone that it stood for Health Ensuring Centre. How clever!

Arjun woke up in a prison cell-like room. The room was off-white and blue in color. He was very terrified. Someone else was also there with him. Their hands were tied in a manner that their backs were touching. The other one was still unconscious. Arjun tried waking him up. He tried pushing him by his shoulders. He also shouted, "Wake Up! Wake up." The other guy finally woke up.

Other guy: Uh! Where am I?

Arjun: If I knew, I would have told you earlier.

Other guy: Oh! My bad. By the way, how did you get here? I was hit by a van and when I opened my eyes, I found myself here.

Arjun: I also met the same incident.

Other guy: You seem furious. What's the reason?

Arjun: It's a long story. I took a break from my daily, monotonous life and decided to meet my childhood friends. I used to live here and then decided to move to a foreign country to join the Defense sector. Besides, I was also going to meet my sister. The last time I saw her was four years ago. But my life is so messed up that now I am here in this damned situation. Besides, I am having a weird feeling in my back.

Other guy: Stop tickling me!

Arjun: I am not tickling you.

Suddenly, a dark black tentacle came shooting out of Arjun's back. An announcement was made in the Center, saying, "Victim-087 has grown tentacles on his back due to the side-effect of the A-Virus or Arachno-Virus."

Other guy: What is that?

Arjun said in a stressful tone: I don't know. It must be our imagination.

Other guy: But how can we both have the same imagi…

Suddenly, the other guy started throwing up blood and became unconscious again. Another announcement was made saying, "Victim-086 has died." Arjun heard some footsteps coming closer. He panicked and tried to stress on the chains as hard as he could.

The team, that was supposed to check the body of Victim-086, was approaching Arjun's cell and suddenly the door of the cell was broken apart by one of the team members. The team found the body lying on the floor in complete silence. One of the team members stepped in. Arjun jumped on him from behind the door and killed that member by piercing his chest with his tentacle. The other members got scared by that gruesome act and ran for their life. Arjun checked the pulse rate of Victim-086 and found out that he was dead. He was terrified but soon he was overwhelmed by a sense of panic as he heard a deafening sound of footsteps coming toward the room.

He quickly came out of the room and four security guards blocked his path. The guards pointed their guns at him and one of them said, "Accept either defeat or death." While Arjun was making eye contact with each of the guards, he silently released his four tentacles and pulled the leg of each guard, making them fall down. As they fell, Arjun said, "Sorry, sir! I decline both defeat and death!" with intense anger and walked away.

As he walked towards the main door of HEC, anyone who came in his way got scared, by Arjun's tentacles coming from behind, and moved out of his way. He came out of the Center and rushed into the metro. One of the HEC staff members quickly tried to inform the Head of the Department, about this monstrous event before Arjun could leave. Meanwhile, The Head of the Department of HEC was sleeping at her home. Her brother was coming from the night shift.

Arjun was frightened. It was almost sunrise. He was walking in the metro while looking backward. There was almost no one in that metro. Someone shouted at him, "Hey!" Arjun panicked and got scared. Out of nervousness, one of his tentacles from the back shot out and pierced through the chest of the man who called out to him. The man died on the spot. It turned out that guy was calling Arjun because he was going to bump into him.

Arjun said to himself in his mind, *I have seen a lot of blood from the moment I kept my feet in Kanpur.* He started getting depressed. He started seeing himself as a monster— a monster that kills others for his personal, pathetic mistakes. Victim-086 could be saved if Arjun had broken the chains in time and focused on him instead of focusing on saving his own life. This man on the metro could have been saved if Arjun hadn't panicked. This scared Arjun even more.

He got remorseful as the sun's rays fell on him and he realized that he made a lot of chaos. As Arjun was walking down the metro, he decided to visit his friend Kartikey. He decided this because his home was closest to the metro station. Besides, Kartikey was a cop, so Arjun was hoping for legal safety. As he walked towards Kartikey's house, his shoe left blood trails to some distance because he, by mistake, must have kept his feet near the dead-body of the man on the metro.

Episode 2

Tag of A Psychopath

The Head of HEC, named Anshika, found out that her brother passed away while coming home from the night shift. She quickly sent the body to the police with a condition that if they managed to find the perpetrator within 24 hours, she would pay them thrice the amount for resolving the mystery. She reached the HEC to find total chaos in it—tables were turned upside down and papers were scattered all around. Anshika exclaimed, "What the hell happened here!"

Her assistant, Savitri, came out from under the table and answered, "Victim-087 under Protocol-C of Arachno-Virus ran away." Savitri further provided the details of the last night's incident. Anshika commanded her to hand over the files containing information about the virus and Victim-087.

The file read details of A-Virus—"Protocol A: Losing consciousness and death within half an hour of the drug being injected into the body. Protocol B: Regaining consciousness after a few hours followed by vomiting up blood and instant death. Protocol C: Regaining consciousness after a few hours, accompanied by thin, long tentacles growing out of the back of the person who has been injected with the drug. The growth of the tentacles is controlled by the emotions of the person, and it can also equip the person with self-healing abilities. Protocol D: Regaining consciousness after being injected, however, there are no significant changes."

It was morning time, and Arjun knocked on the door of Kartikey's house. Kartikey opened the door with a smile on his face. He was surprised to see Arjun and said, "OMG! Arjun! You surprised me!" Arjun was struggling with hiding his agony under a feeble smile. He answered, "A bold surprise for my dumb friend." Kartikey replied, "You haven't changed at all, Arjun."

They both moved inside and Arjun narrated the incident to Karitkey.

Kartikey: Wait! You came from there leaving hundreds of evidence.

Arjun: What kind of evidence?

Kartikey: Uh… Your fingerprints, your shoeprints… everyone at the department must have seen your face and since Kanpur is a developed city now, there are CCTV cameras everywhere.

Arjun: What?

Kartikey: Arjun! You need to erase these evidences.

Arjun: That's why I am here.

Kartikey: How can I help?

Arjun: You are a cop; you should know.

Kartikey said slapping his forehead: You are petrified. You should take some rest. By the way, where is your stuff like suitcases, bags and all?

Arjun: Bro! I gave it to the security guard at the airport so that I wouldn't have to carry it everywhere while I was looking for a cab.

Kartikey: Okay! Please take some rest. I'll bring the luggage on my way from the office to home.

Arjun: Where's your wife?

Kartikey: That headache is in Lucknow.

It was around four in the evening when cops arrived and surrounded Arjun. The cops included Kartikey also. Since Kartikey was bound by his duties; he couldn't protect his friend. The police traced him through the

CCTV present in his way and other evidence. Kartikey said to him, "Sorry, bro! I am stuck. You have to come with us." Arjun was arrested and the very next day, he was going to be presented in front of the judge.

The next day, he was in the courtroom. It turned out that the guy, whom he killed in the metro, was the brother of the Head of Department (HOD) of the HEC, Anshika. As her lawyer summarized the issue to the judge, Arjun started sweating profusely out of fear. Anshika's lawyer was a renowned lawyer of Kanpur, named Arnav Gera. It was clear that the odds were against Arjun this time as the lawyer who was going to handle Arjun's case was an ordinary guy, named Ashish.

Ashish: What is the proof that my client killed her brother?

Arnav: I knew you would ask that. Here, see this CCTV footage.

Arnav showed the footage to prove his point.

(The CCTV footage, in the pen drive, showed Arjun using his tentacles to kill that guy.)

Arnav remarked sarcastically: Any questions?

Ashish was dumbfounded.

Judge: What are these tentacles?

Arnav (to the Judge): My Lord! For that, here are these three files and I would like to call Miss Anshika in the witness box.

(Anshika came into the witness box.)

Arnav: So, Miss Anshika. Is Arjun infected with some sort of virus?

Anshika: Yes, he is.

Ashish: Objection! We need written proof.

Arnav: My Lord! Out of the three files I gave you, one of them contains a file stating Arjun Pandey is infected by Raincoat's Arachno-Virus.

Arjun yelled out of anger: The virus was injected in me forcefully. This all is a pre-planned conspiracy against me!

Judge: Mr. Pandey! Please don't shout and have your seat.

Arnav said, showing a legal document: This document has your fingerprints and states that you took the virus on your own will to cure the intense back pain. My Lord! The files I gave you also contain the declaration and the virus description. The declaration is taken because the virus may be lethal and the person may die. So, this proves that Mr. Arjun Pandey knew it before getting infected.

(They took the fingerprint in the HEC while I was unconscious.)

(Arjun and his lawyer stayed with their mouth open.)

Arnav: But, sir! Don't think that Arjun killed him because of some personal grudge. Let us hear it from Anshika herself.

Anshika: Sir, this virus has a lot of side effects. If you open page three of the file that contains information regarding the Arachno-Virus, just where the statement related to Protocol-D ends, you will find a heading written in bold letters— *"Side Effects"*. Under that heading, the second statement states, "Emotional and Mental Instability under Protocol C". Emotional instability refers to the fact that the mood and emotions of the patient may change anytime. Mental instability means the movements, actions, thought processes, etc., are not in the control of the patient. This all states that Arjun Pandey is a psychopath.

Arnav: Any questions, Mr. Ashish?

Ashish: But how can you prove that he had back pain? There won't be any certificate stating that.

Arnav: Isn't this proof enough to answer all your questions?

Ashish: Answer my question!

Arnav: Ask some logical questions, not absurd ones.

Ashish: This is to the point.

Arnav: You are creating a new point.

Judge: Silence! Please stop fighting, Mr. Ashish! I don't think that any further proof is required to justify the claims. Your point is actually absurd. This court claims Mr. Arjun Pandey to be guilty of the crime but we have decided to release him as he is mentally unstable or a psychopath.

Arjun was despondent. Ashish hesitated in asking for his fee for handling Arjun's case after witnessing the mental trauma evident on Arjun's face. Ashish went away from there without taking the money. Kartikey tried to console him by saying, "Don't worry! You haven't been jailed. This case will surely be a secret."

Arjun and Kartikey moved out of the court into a cab while being captured by the camera of reporters.

Anshika was also being questioned by the media. The media questioned, "Are Raincoat medicines safe?" Anshika answered, "No, we will let you know if we get clarity on the matter."

Arjun and Kartikey decided to go to Arjun's childhood home. On their arrival, the members of the society prevented them from entering the area as everyone now knew that Arjun was a psychopath. Arjun's eyes were glued to a TV in a nearby shop. The news channel reported, "Arjun Pandey also known as Victim-087: The dumbest psycho killer ever. He has been caught within 12 hours of his first attempt to kill." This news was spread all over India. They also showed the media questioning Anshika, which showed Raincoat as innocent in everyone's eyes.

Besides, his home was also burnt by that society's residents in front of Arjun. Arjun saw his childhood getting burnt. He got away from there and received a message on his phone saying, "You have been fired from your job, as we have received information about your mental state." Arjun broke from inside and fell on his knees. Kartikey picked him up and took him to a *rickshaw*. Arjun said to Kartikey, "What was my mistake? Coming here?" as he broke down totally from the inside.

On social media, people criticized Raincoat for producing a dangerous drug that could potentially kill patients. But Raincoat used the power of money to influence famous figures to protect the image of the company; at the same time, it succeeded in blaming Arjun for the unfortunate incidents.

What remained hidden from everyone was that even the judge was corrupt. As a result, there was no charge against Raincoat and Arjun was also released instead of being sent to an asylum.

Episode 3

Beginning of a Killer

It was evening time and the sun had set. Anshika was going home in her car while talking to Savitri on phone.

Anshika: So what happened to the other victims?

Savitri: Victim-085 died under Protocol A and 086 died under Protocol B.

Anshika: Wait! Victim-086 wasn't murdered by 087. Oh! I was almost planning to consult the owner of the Security Department for a code to be mentioned in the files for these special events wherein one victim is killed by another victim before the virus protocol is surely defined.

Savitri: Think of the code as like…

Suddenly, a human body (with eight tentacles coming out of its back), appeared in front of her car and vanished. Anshika shouted, "WHAT THE HELL…!" Petrified, she hit the brakes of the car. Due to the sudden commotion, her phone fell down. She looked here and there but found nothing. She picked up her phone.

Savitri: What happened, ma'am?

Anshika: Nothing! I think that psycho killer was here and I also noticed his tentacles.

Savitri: Are you fine?

Anshika: Yeah! It must be my imagination. I will talk to you later. Bye.

(Anshika declined the call.)

With so many thoughts on her mind, she kept driving. She was thinking about the documentation process and the files that were kept in the bag, which was put in the backseat. She looked into the rear-view mirror to ensure that the files were still there and she didn't forget them in the office. To her surprise, she saw Arjun sitting in the backseat. She was petrified and again hit the brakes of the car. Her head was almost going to bump into the steering wheel but luckily it didn't. She immediately looked back but found the backseat empty. She started sweating profusely out of fear. She slowly dragged her hand towards the handgun in the drawer of the car. She got out of the car with her handgun and searched around the car. She found nothing. She headed towards the car door but she heard the sound of footsteps approaching her from behind. She turned around and saw a stray dog. She asked herself, "How could a dog produce the sound of footsteps!" She convinced herself that it must have been her imagination.

After a few minutes, she was relieved and stopped sweating. When she sat back in the car, she saw Arjun standing in front of her car. Out of fear, she picked up her gun and tried to shoot him. Unfortunately, she marginally missed her target, and the next moment Arjun shot a tentacle, which went piercing through the windshield, her chest, and then the car's seat. The incident occurred at the same place where Arjun's van had met with an accident.

Since cops were busy with many other cases, two newly joined investigators Jaspreet and Sukhbeer were given the case of Anshika. They both were examining the accident scene. They looked at the car and were confused that the whole car was free of dents, cracks, or marks but the windshield and car seat were the only damaged parts. This proved that this wasn't an accident but a pre-planned murder.

They checked Anshika's dead body. There was a hole in her chest and a few cut marks caused by the broken pieces of the windshield. They found her phone and took it to the Cyber Department of police for further investigation.

They check her mobile phone and found out that before dying, she was talking to one of her colleagues named Savitri. Jaspreet proceeded to interrogate Savitri at the department.

Jaspreet: Where did Anshika work?

Savitri: In Raincoat, as HOD of HEC.

Jaspreet: HEC?

Savitri: Health Ensuring Centre. It deals with any complaints filed against the medical staff, hospitals, medicines, etc., working under Raincoat or produced by Raincoat.

Jaspreet: Okay. A sort of customer care service…What are those cell-like rooms for?

Savitri: None of your business. You need to consult some elite person for that.

Jaspreet: Okay! Anshika worked directly under the Head. Am I right?

Savitri: Yeah! She had to look over all the HEC departments all over the world.

Jaspreet: Did Anshika have any enemies?

Savitri: I don't know much but a few days ago she won a case and proved the opposition a psychopath in front of the whole country.

Jaspreet: It must have been a personal case. How did the news spread all over the country?

Savitri: Her sister is a news anchor. She wanted revenge for her brother's death. The opposition guy became a sensation all over the country and 'meme material'. Look at this one 'If you ever feel useless just remember that Arjun Pandey exists'.

Jaspreet: Okay! Who was the lawyer in that case?

Savitri: Kanpur's best and most renowned lawyer Mr. Arnav Gera.

Jaspreet: So, do you know who the opposition was in that case?

Savitri: No, I don't.

Jaspreet: Well! Did Anshika say anything suspicious before death?

Savitri said, interrupting Jaspreet: Ah! Urgent work! I got to go. I have to see all the work of Anshika.

Jaspreet said, turning around, disappointed: Please answer this….Savitri: She saw a guy with eight tentacles.

Here, tell me your email ID. I will email you the call recording.

Jaspreet opted to listen to the recording later. He saw Miss Avantika Sharma (the owner of Raincoat) and Miss Sakshi Gupta (CEO of Raincoat) on his way and decided to talk before meeting Arnav.

Jaspreet: Can you tell me about HEC?

Avantika: Why do you ask?

Jaspreet: The HOD of HEC, Anshika is dead.

Avantika: So, how is her job involved in this?

Jaspreet: It is in our protocol. So, would you tell me about HEC?

Avantika: Sakshi! Tell him about Health Ensuring Centre!

Jaspreet: Wait! I know everything about it. I want to know about those cell-like rooms. What is the need to build prison rooms in a health consultancy service room?

Avantika said, hesitatingly: Uh…

Sakshi: Health Ensuring Centre is also the place where we infect humans with microorganisms, and often, the result could be fatal. So, we have to put them into prison after infection to prevent them from coming out because some become mad psychos which may be lethal if let out.

Jaspreet: It sounds more like a sci-fi horror story because I recently watched one. You know that injecting any drug or anything in someone's body without their permission is illegal.

Sakshi yelled, throwing a pile of legal documents in his face: These documents contain the legal declarations signed by all those patients.

Avantika: Now, instead of teaching me how to do my work, you can get lost!

Avantika and Sakshi went away to handle Raincoat. Jaspreet remained standing there in disappointment looking at all those files scattered here and there.

Jaspreet went on to meet Mr. Arnav Gera.

Jaspreet: Mr. Arnav, Do you know anything about Anshika?

Arnav: Yep! Just a couple of days ago I won her case.

Jaspreet: What was the case about?

Arnav: It was more like an accident but still comes under a murder case. Someone killed her brother by mistake.

Jaspreet: Who was in opposition?

Arnav: A common man named Arjun something. Due to the side effects of a virus, tentacles grow out of his back, more like the famous creepy pasta of Slenderman.

Jaspreet: Is he in jail now?

Arnav: No! We proved him a psychopath. And you know the law.

Jaspreet: Can we have the case file?

Arnav said, handing over the file: Oh, yes!

Jaspreet read the case file which stated, "The case was filed by Miss Anshika Gupta with her lawyer Mr. Arnav Gera against Mr. Arjun Pandey with his lawyer Mr. Ashish. Mr. Arjun has been accused of killing an innocent victim but due to his unstable mental state, he has been released. The government has commanded Raincoat to put a ban on the use of the virus. The judgment is based on a video containing CCTV footage, an explanation by Anshika, a file that contains information related to Arachno-Virus (A-Virus), a file of Arjun Pandey's declaration before getting infected and a file of the medical certificate stating the patient is infected."

Jaspreet said, after skimming through the case file): Can I have a look at the video which is referenced here?

Arnav said, commanding his servant to play the video.

Jaspreet saw the video and finally got to know Arjun Pandey was the one with the tentacles. He could relate that tentacle attack with marks on the windshield, body, and seat. All the links now seemed to add up. Jaspreet now moved on to talk to Arjun too.

Episode 4

Spicy News

Arnav came back to his home after answering Jaspreet. He was exhausted and the moment he opened the door of his house, he looked around at the table. He found a piece of paper saying 'I request you to have a look at the bathroom mirror'. Arnav slowly moved towards the bathroom, taking each step carefully and kicking the door open.

Meanwhile, Jaspreet reached Arjun's place to interrogate him.

Jaspreet: So, Mr. Arjun Pandey! Where were you last night?

Arjun: As usual, chilling at my friend's home.

Jaspreet: Where is your friend's home?

Arjun: The home in which you are currently sitting.

Jaspreet: Where is your home then?

Arjun: Burnt down by society because they think I am a psychopath.

Jaspreet said in a sarcastic tone: Oh, I see!

Arjun asked sarcastically: Do you wanna know who's next?

Jaspreet: Wanna see what it's like to be in jail?

Arjun: Got any solid proof?

Jaspreet: Yeah! This cassette has the video in which you killed Anshika's brother.

Arjun: How funny! There are chances that she could have been killed using a pole or anything like that.

Jaspreet: I know you would say that. Here, listen to this call recording.

Arjun and Jaspreet listened to the call recording. The call recording said, 'I think that I saw the psycho killer with his eight tentacles out'. Jaspreet accused Arjun of being the killer with eight tentacles. . Arjun was shocked and said hesitantly, "Can I listen to it further?" To which, Jaspreet eagerly replied, "Yeah, sure." As they heard it further, they came across the part which said, "It must have been my imagination."

Arjun: She accepted that it was her imagination and she seemed quite stressed. Besides, her brother passed away. Some dumb idiot killed him with eight tentacles. So she is angry and there is a high possibility that it was all a product of her imagination. This makes a lot more sense now.

Jaspreet seemed shocked and angry at the same time.

Arjun: Disappointment always hits hard. Don't worry as you will get used to it.

Jaspreet: We'll see.

Arjun: Door's that side.

Jaspreet's phone started ringing. He received it while leaving Arjun's friend's house. It was Arnav and he wanted Jaspreet to meet him at the earliest. Jaspreet rushed to Arnav's house and found the door open. As he got in, he started calling Arnav's name. Arnav answered him from the bathroom and asked him to come there. He found that the mirror had a message written with blood. The message read, "From Dear Psycho."

Jaspreet said shockingly: So you're next?

Arnav replied angrily: At this moment, you should have asked for security!

Jaspreet: We can't give you security for various reasons and one of the main reasons is that you are not a VIP…

Arnav said, interrupting him: You know who am I? I am the best lawyer in Kanpur.

Jaspreet: Still half of Kanpur doesn't know you. Besides, this case isn't a high-profile case. So, no one would spend their time on it unless you pay all those guards enough money. And by high, I mean in lakhs.

Arnav slapped his forehead in disappointment. Jaspreet left from there without wasting time.

The next evening, Arnav was driving on his way back home. He got a new case of identity forging on that case. His new client had been accused of faking his identity.

Suddenly, someone started firing at Arnav's car. Arnav got scared and tried to gain control of the car. He immediately picked up his phone and called Jaspreet. The call was declined from Jaspreet's side. The phone was charging, so Jaspreet didn't pick it up. Arnav again called Jaspreet. But once again, his call was declined.

Just when all hopes of him were down, he got an idea. To confuse the shooter, Arnav took the other route to his home which involved a police station in between. Just after the turn, Arnav received a phone call from Jaspreet.

Arnav: Hello, Jaspreet!

Jaspreet: Yes! Sorry! I was busy in the toilet and my phone was in charge. Sorry!

Arnav: Anyway! The problem is that someone's firing at my car. Each time I try to look out, he shoots and I dodge the bullets marginally.

Jaspreet: What! Wait! Let me do something.

(Jaspreet cut the call and dialed Arjun's phone number.)

Jaspreet: Where are you, Arjun?

Arjun: At my friend's home.

Jaspreet: Why do I hear firing?

Arjun: Watchin' an action movie. I gotcha appreciate the sound quality though. Isn't it great?

Jaspreet: Yeah! Sure! But, my sweet friend, here's a piece of advice—Anshika and Arnav are not your enemies. Raincoat is your real enemy. Everything started from Raincoat.

(The call got declined.)

The firing stopped at once. The shooter's car also stopped, took a U-turn and drove away from Arnav. Arnav relaxed and continued to drive toward his home.

Suddenly, Arjun appeared in front of his car. Arnav got scared and lost the balance of the car. He crashed the car into a letterbox.

Unfortunately, the letterbox was near a police station and a reporter was also there, who was called there by Arjun. A few moments ago, Arjun, called the reporter and said, "Urge for spicy news? If yes, come to…".

The car crashed and immediately caught the attention of the police and reporter. They rushed towards the car. The reporter asked his cameraman to start recording. The policeman opened the door and Arnav fell out of the car. Arnav got up with help of a policeman. He had no wounds or scratches due to the airbags.

Police: Are you drunk?

Arnav: No. Absolutely not.

Suddenly, there was a rattling sound of a bottle falling. The sound came from the backseat. The sound immediately caught the attention of the policeman. He rushed towards there and opened the door immediately. He first saw nothing due to the darkness, so started checking inside. He felt a liquid container sort of thing in there. He immediately pulled it out. A bottle of an alcoholic beverage by the name Antiquity was found. This raised a reasonable doubt in his mind. Arnav was shocked because he doesn't drink alcohol.

Police: What is this?

Arnav was embarrassed.

Police: I asked what this is!

Meanwhile, the reporter: As you can see that the most reputed and well-known lawyer of Kanpur has been found drunk and driving.

Arnav got shocked by what the reporter said. He immediately handed the fine money to the police and rushed back to his home.

The media spiced up this story by calling the money a bribe. Everyone trusted the media and the media misused it. Well! This was an everyday thing. The news production team added this quote, "Could that same money have been fine if there was a human instead of the letterbox? Is our jurisdiction so hollow and weak? Are our laws allowing any rich fellow to drive like it is his parental property?"

These fake news channels were busy questioning the law. But did they even let the suspect speak? No. Well! No need to be surprised. This was a very common thing then and now too.

Arnav reached home. He found Arjun sitting on his couch and watching TV. The TV was showing the news of Arnav's car accident. In this digital era, the information didn't even take minutes to travel around the globe.

TV reporter: Nobody can be trusted these days! The law protectors turn out to be the lawbreakers! One of the most reputed lawyers, Mr. Arnav Gera was seen drunk and driving...

Arjun said, looking at Arjun: Oh! Mr. Drunkard! No one had this expectation from you. You disappoint us.

Arnav's eyes shifted from watching TV to Arjun with the agony clearly visible on his face.

Arnav: You ruined my damn life in a blink. You, son of a...

Arjun: Oh really! Just check your WhatsApp, Facebook, and other social media accounts. No one trusts you now. Everyone is cursing you. They know me as a psychopath. A psychopath doesn't have this much brain **OR DOES HE?**

Arnav checked his phone and broke down emotionally. People were saying, "You are trash in the name of a lawyer", "Our law system is messed up because of people like you", "If I sue a lawyer, will he need one for himself?", "Since LHS = RHS, therefore LAW = BLIND", etc., to him on social media.

Arjun took out his gun while wearing a glove and kept it on the table in front of Arnav.

Arnav got depressed by every notification. A variety of humiliating curses in different languages, and memes were all over his Facebook homepage.

Arnav picked up the gun and pointed it at Arjun. Arnav, with an evil smile, said "Aw! So innocent you are, aren't you? You thought that I would go into depression and kill myself. People will say today, tomorrow, and even the day after tomorrow but after some time they will forget. The thing that remains is the legal procedure. I paid the fine. I crashed and showed no signs of being drunk. But soon, Arjun, you will be crying because you have been proven a psychopath legally. People trust legal documents."

Suddenly his phone rang and he picked up. As he put the phone at his ear, his evil smile turned into a shock-filled frown. He replied, "WAIT! NO! NO! I CAN EXPL…" but the phone got declined before he could speak further. The phone fell from his hand. His body vibrated as that mental shock shook him from inside.

He knelt down in depression. He looked upwards and said, "No one trusts me now. No one. Not even my wife." He looked towards Arjun and put the gun on his forehead. The gunshot sound echoed through the whole house.

Episode 5

Let's Remove the Obstacle

Jaspreet and his team were investigating the area of Arnav's death in the morning. He carefully looked at the scene. The gun was in Arnav's hand, which clearly meant this was a suicide but Jaspreet was not ready to believe it. He spotted the phone and hid it in Arnav's pocket. He hid it because he thought that the last phone call was from him due to which Jaspreet would become one of the suspects and might lose his job.

Arjun also reached there with a present. Arjun saw the body of Arnav and made eye contact with Jaspreet.

Arjun: Mr. Arnav! What happened to you?

Jaspreet: He is in sleep forever. What are you doing here?

Arjun: Today is his birthday. Just came to give him a present.

Jaspreet: How do you know Arnav?

Arjun: Do you still think that half of Kanpur doesn't know him?

Arjun showed fake disappointment on his face. He moved towards the door a little, turned around for a moment and said, "Next is Sakshi. Someone will die before tonight. And besides, Anshika, Arnav and whoever thinks of me as a psychopath are my enemy. The fella who gave me this tip extended my revenge and he is the responsible one now." Arjun ended his dialogue with a devil-like smile and moved away.

Jaspreet thought to investigate the area more before leaving for Sakshi's house. Jaspreet found a hidden camera which was placed in such a way that it must have recorded what happened at the moment of suicide.

Jaspreet proceeded to play the recording of the camera. The recording showed a man coming in from a window, turning on the TV and sitting on the couch to watch the news. A few minutes later, the recording showed Arnav coming into the house with a frightened face. The video continued and showed Arnav turning on his phone, kneeling down, the man taking out a gun, Arnav pointing the gun at the man, receiving a call, and finally shooting himself. The man carefully exited the scene without leaving any marks. No footprints. No fingerprints. In this whole video, the man didn't even turn back toward the camera once.

But when the man was going towards the door, he looked at Arnav's body. His face was half visible but was quite afar. Jaspreet zoomed in but the footage pixelated. The investigation came out with no solid evidence.

Jaspreet reached Sukhbeer, who was in Kartikey's cabin discussing another case with Kartikey. Jaspreet called Sukhbeer.

Jaspreet: Sukhbeer! I think that Arnav is very closely linked to Anshika's case.

Sukhbeer: How?

Jaspreet: The presence of Arjun. Arjun came today to give a birthday present to Arnav and said to me sarcastically that the next victim is Sakshi.

Sukhbeer: This is very loose evidence and isn't strong enough to support the case.

Jaspreet: But you know! What goes into investigating?

Sukhbeer: Then how will we tell others that Sakshi is linked in this case?

Jaspreet: Before Arnav's current case, Arnav was handling Sakshi's case. We can make up this lie.

Kartikey was standing behind and remembered that Arjun had asked him to prevent Sukhbeer from coming with Jaspreet. Kartikey suddenly called Sukhbeer.

Kartikey: Wait, Sukhbeer! You'll have to go with me for the investigation.

Jaspreet: He is busy. He's going with me.

Before Kartikey could say further, Jaspreet took Sukhbeer with him. Jaspreet said to Sukhbeer, "We must hurry. Sakshi will be home any time and we must protect her life." This was the golden chance to catch Arjun and kill him on the spot.

Kartikey got tensed that how could he stop Sukhbeer and then saw his servant. He grabbed his servant, gave the gun to the servant and fired it. The gun was fired such that the servant died on the spot and Kartikey got injured. The gunshot echoed through the whole station.

Sukhbeer left Jaspreet upon hearing the sound of a gunshot. Sukhbeer rushed to Kartikey and Jaspreet rushed to Sakshi's house. Other policemen and Sukhbeer came to Kartikey.

Sukhbeer: What happened, sir?

Kartikey: He tried to kill me but ended up killing himself.

Sukhbeer: Hey! Make the jeep ready. We are going to the hospital.

Meanwhile, Jaspreet rushed and reached Sakshi's house. He tried to open the door but it was locked. He broke the door open aggressively. Before stepping in, he took his gun out and moved in without making a sound. He searched the house by looking here and there.

On a few steps from the door, he stepped on a piece of paper lying on the floor. The paper read, "The floor above." He looked up and found the door of the room upstairs was open. Jaspreet carefully walked upstairs and entered the room which had "Over Here" written on the door. There was a cross in the middle of the room.

The room was a work room of Sakshi. There was a bench that had a photo frame showing a photo of Sakshi and Avantika playing together in childhood. Jaspreet threw the photo frame which landed directly on the cross and nothing happened.

Jaspreet walked towards the cross. Still, nothing happened. He finally stood on the cross. He looked towards his side and saw Arjun jumping towards him but Jaspreet caught Arjun by the neck and threw him towards the almirah. He fell on the almirah and it broke.

Meanwhile, Sakshi was in the office and talking to the HOD of the Inventory and Management Department (IMD). Every six months, the files needed to be revised, which actually meant, in their code language, that the files had to be stored as both softcopy in the supercomputer COAT (Computational Organizing and Assisting Technology) and as hardcopy in the storeroom of Raincoat. This was done under Sakshi's supervision.

Sakshi: We have revised the inventory. We will update you by evening.

She put the phone back and looked at Savitri who came in place of Anshika for HEC files. Savitri took them to Sakshi before to the Data Department for the Revision Protocol.

Savitri: What about the revised file of the Health Ensuring Centre?

Sakshi: Oh yeah! It's done.

She checked her bag for the file but couldn't find it. She remembered that she signed them in the morning in her kitchen and must have left them on the dining table. Sakshi said, "Sorry to say but the folder is at home. Just give me some time, Savitri! My home is a few minutes away from here." Sakshi quickly closed her bag and rushed towards her home.

Meanwhile, at Sakshi's home, Arjun got up and his eyes were trying to find the axe. The axe was brought by Arjun in order to remove this obstacle named Jaspreet. Arjun's eyes finally found it. But before he could throw the axe, Jaspreet picked up a screwdriver from his work desk of Sakshi and threw the screwdriver, which pierced partly into Arjun's hand and later into the wall. His hand got stuck on the wall due to the screwdriver. The pain was easily visible in his eyes.

While Arjun removed the screwdriver, Jaspreet made his gun ready. As Arjun removed the screwdriver, Jaspreet pointed the gun at Arjun and ordered him to put his hands up. Arjun put his hands up. Jaspreet said, "Now, I'm gonna call Sukhbeer" and searched for the phone but couldn't find it. Arjun said, "Finding this?" and pulled the phone out of his jacket.

Jaspreet: Well played?

Arjun: Ahhhh! (He screamed in pain while holding his bleeding hand.) There are five stages of grief.

Jaspreet: I know that same old line. Someone else already added a sixth one.

Arjun: I went through none of them because I went through extreme mental instability due to that virus.

Ahhhh! But the only thing that keeps me stable is the horror when I saw that in the Centre that night.

Jaspreet: Tell me what you saw in HEC! I may be able to help.

Arjun: No, you can't. Ahhhh! Because one day, Raincoat and its clever CEO will buy you all. Just go and ask them what happened to Victim-088. They will tell that he must have died due to the virus. The reality is he survived the virus without any side effects but he was shot dead by Raincoat Faculty members before he could reveal the truth in front of everyone.

Jaspreet: Got any proof?

Arjun: I am the biggest proof.

Jaspreet: Well! You know… You can't do anything. They are too powerful.

Arjun: That's what I said earlier. You must also have been bought by Raincoat.

Jaspreet: No, I am not.

Arjun: Yes, you are.

This yes-no continued further. Jaspreet got angry and fired two bullet shots at Arjun (one on the unharmed hands and one on the stomach). Arjun shouted in agony and fell down. Jaspreet smiled and turned around.

Arjun called Jaspreet and said, "Hey! My death won't be this easy." He stood up and removed the bullets from his wounds. His wounds started healing themselves and he said, "The virus gave me healing powers too. I can heal myself whenever I want." By the end of this statement, he snapped the hand which had the wound from the screwdriver and the wound vanished after the snap. Arjun said, "You thought I was screaming in agony? I need to appreciate my acting skills though."

Jaspreet was shocked and pointed the gun at Arjun. Arjun used his tentacle to snatch the gun. The tentacle went furiously, hit Jaspreet's hand, and successfully snatched the gun from Jaspreet. Arjun now pointed the gun at Jaspreet. He sweated in fear. He soon turned back and ran away to save his life. Arjun purposely shot the gun on the wall to scare Jaspreet.

As soon as Jaspreet reached the stairs, Arjun pulled the leg of Jaspreet through his tentacle. Jaspreet fell down the stairs and Sakshi opened the door. She was surprised to see the chaos. Jaspreet stood up and walked towards Sakshi. He said, "Arjun was making a trap for you in…" and before he could say further, Arjun shot four bullets at him. Jaspreet was dead instantly and Sakshi was shocked.

Arjun descended the staircase and on reaching the middle of the staircase, he and Sakshi saw each other. Arjun tried to run back but Sakshi pulled the shotgun from the wall and shot at Arjun's leg. *It seems like the shotgun was not for decoration.* Arjun fell down the staircase due to a shot. He couldn't heal himself because the bullet was too deep inside and was blocking the re-healing process.

Arjun somehow pulled himself up the stairs through his tentacles. Sakshi tried rushing to him but couldn't run fast because of the heavy shotgun. He escaped through the window on the floor above. Sakshi looked outside the window and shot at Arjun's tentacle. He was trying to swing like a spider but ended up falling due to her shot.

She came outside to catch Arjun red-handed but he was missing. She came back to Jaspreet's body and called the police to clean the mess. She went inside and got very confused by seeing the mess caused. She asked herself, "Why is the almirah broken? Why is there so much blood over there? Why is there a hole in the wall? What the hell was going on here?" She wasn't able to go back to the office and thought to give the file tomorrow to Savitri.

Episode 6

CEO Execution

Avantika entered her office and took a seat. She found a letter kept in the middle of her desk. The letter stated, "From VICTIM-087" in place of the address. The letter said, "Dear Avantika, with great displeasure I would like to inform you that your beloved CEO, Miss Sakshi Gupta, is my next target. She won't be able to see the sun tomorrow in Kanpur." She called Sakshi to confess to her on this.

Avantika: Sakshi! Have a look at this letter.

Sakshi read the letter and got slightly shocked. She closed the letter and when she read the name of the sender, she was dumbfounded.

Sakshi: Victim-087? We use victim code-word for HEC-subjected victims only.

Sakshi pulled the revised HEC file. Avantika came near her. They both found Victim-087 in it and also found his real name was Arjun. By hearing the name Arjun, Sakshi remembered yesterday's incident at her house when Jaspreet said, "Arjun was planning a trap."

Sakshi: I think I know this guy!

Avantika: How?

Sakshi summarized everything.

Avantika: What was the trap for you?

Sakshi: I don't know. I think Jaspreet fell into all those traps and died. The blood marks must have been of him.

Avantika: This time our enemy is quite bold and stubborn.

Sakshi: Will money shut him up?

Avantika: If it was only about money, why would he have killed the investigator?

Sakshi: What should we do now?

Avantika thought for a while and said: Want a vacation!

Sakshi: Oh! Yeah! What about the Maldives?

Avantika booked a plane for Sakshi. The plane would have a very limited crew including two pilots, two hostesses and a cook with his two boys. The crew members would have an ID card with their photos, details and a QR code. The QR code would only allow access. The plane's destination wouldn't be told to any crew member until the plane completed half the journey. The plane fuel accessories were filled as if it would be a quite long flight, in case there was a change in the plan.

It was noon and the crew was on their way. One of the boys of the cook got stuck in traffic. Kartikey was standing in place of the traffic policemen; he actually fooled the real traffic policeman and took his position. As the boy was getting late, he shouted, "Can't you just let me go?" While he shouted outside, his ID card showed Raincoat's logo. Kartikey found him and told him to go the other way round because the road was jammed due to an accident.

The boy took the other route. While the boy was taking the other route, he looked in the mirror to find someone sitting in the back seat. He stopped the car and immediately looked behind. He found no one. As he looked in front, someone choked him by pressing his neck against the car seat using a leather belt. He tried to help himself but ended up pulling the gear into reverse. The car bumped and his head hit the steering wheel very hard. He died on the spot due to the impact on his head.

The killer was none other than Arjun himself. He took the body out and dressed as the boy. He took the ID card and placed a temporary lamination cover type layer which had the photo in middle. It covered the photo of the boy with the photo of Arjun.

Arjun reached the plane in which Sakshi would go. He entered the area. The ID card's QR and face were checked. Luckily, no one recognized him. He entered the plane successfully.

The first thing he did was he took two glasses of water for the pilots and mixed a few drugs that would cause them to sleep. This drug would take at least 15-30 minutes to work. He took the glasses to the cockpit. The pilots took a sip and continued to check the plane.

The cook called him. Sakshi had already placed an order. The hostesses were checking that Sakshi was comfortable. The pilots made themselves sure of everything. The plane was ready to take off. But suddenly, an officer came to a stop. He rushed into the plane and said, "These are updated files of weather conditions. A storm was approaching but it has changed direction. The plane can take the east route over the River Ganga." The plane took off.

Meanwhile, the security team of the plane was checking the IDs. Suddenly, they found an ID that had a secondary photo pasted over the real photo.

They checked it twice and go shocked. They rushed to investigate the plane but it was taking off. The plane couldn't be stopped because the time of it landing back would have taken more time.

They informed the in charge of the flight plan. He said, "Avantika ma'am was correct. Let me inform one of the hostesses. Those hostesses are trained mercenaries." One of the hostesses was informed about this.

As Arjun was changing his jacket, he dropped the drug bottle. The other cook boy saw him and found it suspicious. He said, "What was that?" and got scared by the way Arjun looked at him. Before he could run away, Arjun used his tentacle to kill him by penetrating it through his abdomen. The boy died instantly as the tentacle came out of his mouth and no scream was made.

As he dragged the body to hide, a hostess appeared in front of him. Arjun shot his tentacle to kill her but she caught the tentacle and pulled Arjun. He hit the wall and fell to the ground. She put one of her feet on his chest. She said, "What did ya think?" Arjun was shocked by her skills.

Arjun: I thought of teaching someone a lesson.

Hostess: Stop dreaming!

Arjun: Okay, then! I will show it practically.

Arjun pulled her feet and she fell down. He got up, picked her up with his tentacles, and threw her. She fell right beside Sakshi. Sakshi got up from her seat and got shocked. She said, "Oh! So, we meet again." He replied, "Yeah! Sure! Last time was unplanned but this time everything is planned." She took out her gun and pointed her gun at him.

He replied, "Just try shooting." Sakshi put her gun down but shot at his leg, where he was shot by shotgun last time. Arjun pretended to be harmed but then looked at Sakshi and took the bullet from him. She was shocked. He said, "Want to see what else I can do?" and used his tentacle to pierce through the lying hostesses. The hostesses screamed in pain as he threw her sideways. Sakshi was frightened by the scene.

The other hostess threw a rod which pierced through Arjun's hand. Arjun felt the pain because the rod was blocking his hand from healing. Sakshi smiled at seeing him in deep agony. The hostess hit Arjun, pushed him into another compartment of the plane and closed the door. They both could see him through the tiny window on the door.

They both laughed at seeing him struggle with the rod. The shouts of agony filled joy and a feeling of relief in them.

But they got confused when they saw Arjun looking out the window and laughing. Arjun finally removed the rod from him. He was now laughing at them. Soon, the other hostess called Sakshi to look outside. The view outside showed the plane descending quite steeply.

The hostess rushed to see the cockpit and was shocked to find the pilot unconscious. She shouted from the cockpit about this to Sakshi. The plane touched the waters of the Holy River Ganga before Sakshi could take any decision.

The debris of the plane was floating here and there. Arjun managed to get out of the plane and the river due to his healing powers and tentacles. Everyone else on the plane was dead.

Arjun reached home and met Kartikey.

Arjun: Bro! She won't see the sun tomorrow.

Kartikey: Great! I think this is enough.

Arjun: No! No! Not at all! I don't want someone else to go through the same fate as mine.

Kartikey: When did you start being so Samaritan?

Arjun: Bro! Two nightmares made me think like that. Remember I told you about Victim-088 who was shot even though he survived the virus? He was our friend Naveen. This is one nightmare and the other nightmare is about my sister. If she comes here, she might also go through the same fate as mine. These two nightmares don't let me sleep.

Kartikey: You know I never understood how it feels to be betrayed but still I will help you in the name of a decades-old friendship.

Arjun: That's my boy! Now, let's watch TV.

Kartikey turned on the TV. The news channels showed the news of the plane crash stating, "The CEO of one of the most trusted pharmaceutics Raincoat, named Miss Sakshi Gupta has died. There are no traces of the plane at any airport. Is this Miss Avantika Sharma's plan?" One of the reporters was shown interviewing Avantika.

Reporter: Do you know anything about this flight, Miss?

Avantika: Yeah! I do.

Reporter: That means you are responsible for her death.

Avantika: No! She was supposed to go on a vacation.

Reporter: Then why is there no mention of this flight in any record of any airport?

Avantika: This was supposed to be a confidential flight. The flight had some important files.

Reporter: What about her vacation?

Avantika: Because of the whole procedure…

Reporter: Please wait! Our sources found a man entered the plane mischievously. Now, the question still remains. ***Why did he kill her? Was he paid by someone? Why? How? Who?*** There are many such questions. To stay updated, stay with us and our news channel.

Episode 7

Avantika Backfires

Avantika was in deep grief due to the death of Sakshi. She was not only the CEO but also a childhood friend of hers from school. They started this corporation together but since it was the dream of Avantika, she was claimed to be the founder. Sakshi was a professional in management, so, she took the post of CEO. She was getting flashbacks of her childhood in her mind.

Suddenly, Savitri entered to call her outside.

Savitri: Ma'am! You need to come outside. People are at the peak to protest. And yesterday, that tentacle monster entered HEC and didn't cause chaos but did photography.

Avantika: Photography? We will discuss that later. For now, what is happening outside?

Savitri: That psychopath is revealing the secrets of HEC.

Avantika reached outside and found Arjun wearing a mask. He had convinced a large number of the public that Raincoat experimented on humans. Arjun said to Avantika in front of the whole public, "So, Miss Avantika Sharma! Have a look at these photos," and showed photos of the inside of HEC.

Avantika soon realized that these were photos of the HEC. Avantika moved a little in front and said, "Would you trust a psychopath?" and snatched the mask off Arjun. She revealed in front of everyone that he was that psycho, Victim-087. But Arjun shouted in front of the public.

Arjun: I may be a psycho but the photos?

Avantika: Editing… Photoshop… You know the stuff.

Arjun: What about those vans?

Avantika: It is part of an upcoming plan for a mobile consultancy.

Arjun: And what about…

A random guy from the public shouted, "Don't over-exaggerate. You are a psycho and you did what you would. *Foolishness*. What else could we have expected?"

The whole public also shouted, *"**Foolishness!**"* The public realized they had been fooled and left the place immediately. Arjun tried to call the people but no one listened due to the prejudice they had.

Avantika was proceeding to her office. Suddenly, the HOD of Security came with a file and started talking with her.

Mohini (HOD of Security): Please revise this file!

Avantika: I almost forgot this is Arjun Pandey's case. Now, I'll have to handle the tasks of Sakshi until someone else takes her place.

They both reached the office. Suddenly, Mohini's phone started ringing. She picked up the call and started conversing.

Mohini: Yeah! You can go to Arjun's house but be careful with that rumor thing.

She declined the call. Avantika was confused after hearing the statement.

Avantika: Arjun?

Mohini: Oh! Yeah! His name is also Arjun Pandey.

Avantika: Can I see a photo of him?

Mohini: Yeah, but why?

Avantika: Quite curious.

Mohini: Okay! Then.

Mohini showed a photo of Arjun and Mohit to Avantika. Avantika didn't even take seconds to realize it was the same Arjun Pandey codenamed by them as Victim-087. Avantika thought a little. She later commanded Mohini.

Avantika: Call you brother right now?

Mohini: What happened?

Avantika: I said call him!

Mohini called her brother. She was quite frightened and worried while talking to her. Her brother rushed there and reached there in under 15 minutes.

Mohit: What happened, *Didi*?

Mohini: Not me! Ma'am called you.

Mohit: Yes, Ma'am.

Avantika: What work do you do?

Mohit: I am in the army.

Avantika: Oh I see! The news is that I am firing your sister.

Mohit and Mohini: What!

The siblings were frightened and looked anxious.

Avantika: Mohit! You can save her job.

Mohit: How?

Avantika: Do you know any Arjun Pandey?

Mohit: Yes!

Avantika: You have to kill him.

Mohini: Wait! No!

Mohit interrupted Mohini and said: Okay! Done!

Avantika: Good! As a friend, you must be knowing how to execute him. Am I right?

Mohit: Yeah! (let out a sigh of grief)

Mohit and Mohini walked out of the cabin. He looked at her with grief on his face. He called her and said…

Mohit: Didi! Today is the last day we are meeting.

Mohini: Why?

Mohit: Arjun is infected with a virus that causes tentacles to come out of his back. There is no chance that I can beat him.

Mohini: You should try talking to him.

Mohit: It is about your career. And the fate he has gone through, he will kill anyone who tries to jeopardize his plan.

Savitri came from behind and handed over a bag. She said, "This bag has a syringe that can stop the tentacles for half an hour. This bag also has a suit. If you don't want Arjun to know that his friend is killing him, you can wear this suit to hide your face." Mohit stood speechless for a few minutes.

Kartikey had gone to work and Arjun was planning for the execution of Avantika on the whiteboard. The plan was like this—"Avantika will leave for her house at this time and her car will come at this time. So, if Arjun catches the driver at the correct time, he will be able to get into the car and Mohit will be right there at the…".

Suddenly, Arjun heard a breaking noise. He immediately went to the door and saw a man standing in a mercenary-type dress.

Arjun: Sorry! There are no pests in our house, sir.

Mohit: I can see the same humor even after so many years. I've been sent from Raincoat to tell you to stop the chaos you've been causing.

Arjun: The voice seems familiar. Is that Mo…

Mohit: Don't change the topic! Surrender now!

Arjun: Ah! You can't even let say me anything.

Mohit: We gave you time for negotiation.

Arjun: When? Nowadays, nowhere a suspect is negotiated. The news media is always there as a substitute. They come to a conclusion before the actual law does, whether you are a criminal or not.

Mohit: I got to agree with that but you are trying to again to change the topic again.

Arjun sighed and said: A stubborn one… So, here goes another kill in my name.

He shot one of his tentacles at him. Mohit caught the tentacle, pulled Arjun, held him by the neck, and was almost going to inject the injection but he stopped. Arjun said, "What happened? Got scared?" Mohit got angry and instantly injected the fluid with the injection and threw him on the table. Arjun fell on the table and broke it.

Arjun tried to stand up but he was hallucinating. He stood up and tried to look at Mohit but his dizziness couldn't see properly. Mohit hit him again and Arjun fell again. After a few minutes, he was in his senses again.

He tried to shoot four of his tentacles. The tentacles went shooting fast but suddenly fell to the ground. They shrank back into his back. Arjun was shocked and said, "What the hell is happening!" Mohit replied, "I infected a fluid which will stop those tentacles for half an hour." Arjun threw a piece of a broken table at Mohit. Mohit dodged the piece by blocking it with his hands and saw Arjun running outside the house. Mohit came behind him.

Arjun bumped into the van of Raincoat and said, "Raincoat has released me. I need to take quick action." He came outside and saw his neighbor's bike with the keys in it. Without waiting for a moment, he sat on the bike of his neighbor and zoomed off. The neighbor came out and shouted from behind, "You idiot! The brakes are not working!"

Mohit sat in the van, turned it on and rushed behind Arjun. From behind, the neighbor was scared by the Raincoat van which went past him. He shouted again, "Hey, van guy! Don't you know about the speed limit!"

Mohit found three knives in the drawer of the Raincoat van. He thought that bullets were too less to use. He threw a knife at Arjun and tried not to lose control of the van. The knife went flying and missed Arjun marginally.

Mohit made a disappointed face. But without a second thought, he threw the next knife. The knife went flying, missed Arjun again and hit a tree's branch. The branch broke and fell on the van. Though it didn't break the windshield, it almost made him lose control of the van.

Mohit thought again, fixed his aim and threw the knife. The knife flew and hit Arjun right his back. Arjun lost his balance and fell off the bike. Arjun managed to stand up immediately. Mohit tried to hit Arjun with the van but missed and the van went a lot far because of the high speed. Arjun picked himself and the bike. He continued to drive. Mohit took a sharp turn and continued to follow Mohit.

Mohit took out his gun and started shooting at Arjun. Arjun somehow dodged the bullets by riding in a zigzag way. Mohit ran out of bullets. Arjun was happy to see his gun empty. The happiness didn't last long. He bumped into a truck because the brakes of the bike were already broken.

Arjun fell down at a distance. His head was completely bleeding and wounds covered his body. He was unconscious instantly. Mohit got out of the van, picked up Arjun's body and kept it in the van. They moved towards Raincoat. Mohit said to himself, "Never thought that I would take revenge for a small betrayal in childhood, in this way. Anyways, no way he could have survived. My friend, sorry for everything but I was constrained and so were you."

They got stuck in traffic at many places and the time of the fluid (injected in Arjun) ran out. Arjun's body was unconscious but he was alive and so was the virus inside of him. The virus healed his body, curing his small wounds and especially his head. One of his tentacles came out and slowly moved toward the engine.

The virus had a special ability to show intelligence but only when the host's brain was not properly working or was at a vulnerable stage. The virus had enough intelligence that it also needed to save its host in order to survive, so the virus was healing Arjun's injuries (even the internal ones) and was trying to save Arjun.

Mohit was waiting at the green signal. He decided to smoke some cigarettes. As soon as he lit the lighter, his lighter fell down and when someone pressed the horns from behind, he realized that the signal was green. He didn't pay much attention to the lighter because the light became green.

The tentacle came from behind. It slowly surrounded the lighter and tightly held it. It proceeded slowly toward the engine.

Suddenly, the van blasted. Mohit fell at a distance and died on the spot. The van was soon covered in flames and Arjun came out of the flames. He tried to run away before the crowd surrounded the van. Arjun found Mohit. He removed the mask in curiosity and realized that it was Mohit. He checked his bag and found the jacket he gifted him in childhood. Arjun cried tearlessly in grief.

Episode 8

The Sad Ending

It was almost nighttime when Arjun came back home. The neighbor was cursing Kartikey because Arjun took his bike. Arjun returned the bike to the neighbor and apologized.

Kartikey: Where were you Arjun?

Arjun: I will tell you tomorrow morning. I am quite tired.

The sun had risen. A new day and a new beginning *but I see no difference.* Arjun woke up and Kartikey asked him questions related to last night.

Kartikey: Where were you yesterday?

Arjun: Okay! Let me explain slowly and elaborately.

Kartikey: Go ahead!

Arjun: Hey, Kartikey! Remember that Mohit?

Kartikey: Yeah! He used to beat you jokingly and you used to take it seriously.

Arjun: I once cheated in an exam and by that, I got the medal. He started to see me as a villain since then. Then after graduation, we were on our ways. I think the fire was still within and someone fuelled it.

Kartikey: What? You mean…

Arjun: He is no more.

Kartikey: Wait! What happened to him?

Arjun: I killed him.

Kartikey: Was he not going to help us in Avantika's execution?

Arjun: He would have helped but someone filled his ears with lies.

Kartikey: Tell me the whole thing!

Arjun summarized everything.

Kartikey: What are you gonna do next?

Arjun said furiously: I am gonna kill Avantika right in her office.

Kartikey: Stop right there. Arjun! Wait! Take decisions with your mind not with your heart.

Arjun left the house and didn't listen to Kartikey once. He was in a rage. Mohit was an enemy to him but also a vital part of his past.

Kartikey rushed to the door but Arjun rushed towards the bus stop. Kartikey was disappointed. He suddenly got a call from Sukhbeer.

Sukhbeer: Sir, we have a golden chance to catch Victim-087. Avantika has initiated this plan. For this, we have to reach Raincoat. According to her plan, one of her friends was killed by him and in rage, he must be coming to Raincoat.

Kartikey: Okay! Move! I am on the way.

Arjun was on his way to Raincoat. He took the bus which had one stop near Raincoat. Suddenly, the bus stopped at a stop on a bridge. The stop had a police team on their way to find Arjun. One policeman came in to check the bus passengers with a photo. The photo was taken by Mohit and when Arjun was unconscious. The policeman glanced at all the passengers at once. Then once again and found Arjun.

He proceeded towards Arjun and asked, "Where are you going, sir?" Arjun replied, "To Raincoat. I am an employee." The policemen replied, "Or for a kill?" and showed him the photo. Arjun tried to kill him with his tentacle but missed marginally. The policeman grabbed him by his collar and threw him to the ground. Arjun pulled his leg and made him fall. He rushed to the bus. And before the policeman was able to catch him, he jumped off the bridge instantly.

He landed on a bus that was going parallel to the bridge. The bus had already passed the previous stop but it stopped at the next stop. The police team checked the bus both inside and at the top. To their disappointment, Arjun was still missing. He already used his tentacle to get over the bus on the bridge.

He soon reached Raincoat and deceived the guards. He stormed into Avantika's cabin. Avantika was not there. Instead, a message was written on the window saying "Meet us at terrace".

Arjun rushed to the terrace. There he found Avantika sitting in a helicopter.

Avantika: Quite late? Aren't you?

Arjun: Why were you waiting for me then? Is there some attraction?

Avantika: Why are standing then? Are you afraid?

Arjun proceeded towards Avantika. As Arjun took a few steps, Kartikey and Sukhbeer came from both sides of Arjun. Kartikey moved forward and pointed the gun at Arjun's forehead. Arjun knelt down.

Arjun: Why didn't I become blind before seeing this day?

Kartikey: Then make everyone else.

Kartikey moved his jacket in such a way that the flashbang on his belt was visible to Arjun. Kartikey did this purposely to help Arjun without getting noticed by others. Arjun understood the sign of Kartikey and punched him, such that the flashbang fell and exploded. Everyone got blinded for some time. At that time, a gunshot was heard and Avantika's helicopter flew away. Everyone thought that Arjun was shot and Avantika peacefully went away.

As the blindness went away, Kartikey and Sukhbeer found a body lying. They both turned the body and found out it was the helicopter's pilot. After realizing this, Arjun took away the helicopter. Sukhbeer was worried and disappointed whereas Kartikey was happy but wasn't showing his emotions and avoiding any suspicion. Meanwhile, Avantika was relaxing in the helicopter.

Avantika: Finally, out of this chaos.

Arjun: Where would you like to go?

Avantika: Anywhere but far from here.

Arjun: Let's go to hell.

Avantika realized what was happening and immediately pulled out her knife. Arjun said, "Sit back and the journey will be…" and suddenly Avantika put her knife on Arjun's neck.

Meanwhile, when Sukhbeer got angry as he couldn't catch Arjun again, he started shooting at the helicopter and ended up destroying both the rotors of the helicopter. The helicopter was almost out of control but Arjun sent out his eight tentacles to gain control of the helicopter. Arjun had only eight tentacles, but now he couldn't use any of them or the helicopter would crash.

Avantika: Why are you doing this?

Arjun: I want vengeance and revenge. You all proved me a psychopath in front of the whole world. My life is now like a stray dog. I only get hate from everyone.

Avantika: You have killed so many people till now. Isn't that enough for revenge?

Arjun: Oh! Every day I walk on the streets, every third person calls me a psychopath. Out of my all childhood friends, only one trusts me. That is Kartikey. They burnt my childhood house. They fired me from my job because I am a psychopath. I had one sister and she doesn't know about this. I don't want her to go through all this. **Staying in jail is a better option than being called a psychopath.**

Avantika: Oh! That's pretty sad. How can one stop if it is your luck?

Arjun: Luck? Now, see this.

Arjun pushed Avantika back and all the tentacles came back. He crashed the helicopter into Raincoat's building, right in Avantika's cabin. Avantika managed to jump out of the helicopter at the right moment. The helicopter crashed through the Raincoat's building.

Avantika got up and smiled, thinking that Arjun was dead. As Avantika turned back, Arjun appeared behind her and said, "I can't die this easy." She replied, "Oh! Then look behind." Arjun said, "What's there!" and turned back. As he turned back, Avantika pushed Arjun.

Arjun fell towards the center of the Raincoat building at the floor from a height of around 15 floors. As Arjun fell, he saw Sakshi coming from behind Avantika and looking at him fall. Sakshi survived the plane crash because she was never in that plane. It was another girl who was dressed and made her look like Sakshi. Arjun got to know about this plane from Mohit, who the information from Mohini, whereas, Mohini got the information from Avantika.

Arjun fell down and a pole pierced through Arjun's chest, right in the middle. There he took his last breath and in his last moments, he shouted, "There is no good ending other than death itself", which echoed throughout the building.

Kartikey watched the horror as the blood from Arjun filled the carving in the floor shaped like Raincoat's logo. The triangle and the parallelogram above were also filled with blood.

While Arjun took his last breath, he wore the jacket he found in Mohit's bag. This jacket was kept as a showpiece in a museum by the name "Remains of First Publically Roaming Lab-Mutated Human aka Victim-087." Raincoat used this jacket to show their terror. Everything continued how it was going in this world.

Raincoat also changed its logo. Instead of all figures being white, now the above triangle and parallelogram were blood red just to show their terror to everyone. The terror continued and Victim-087 was forgotten for good Raincoat now had a clean and horrifying image in the market and in front of the whole.

Everything continued how it was going. Six months later, the showpiece was stolen from the museum. There was chaos in the museum. One security guard almost caught the thief and asked who you are. He replied "I am Ra… Ra… Rajero…